091959

Reiser, Lynn
Bedtime cat

BEDTIME CAT

by LYNN REISER

GREENWILLOW BOOKS, NEW YORK

13.95

Watercolors and a black
pen were used for the
full-color art.
The text type is
Helvetica Light.

Greenwillow Books,
a division of William
Morrow & Company, Inc.,
105 Madison Avenue,
New York, NY 10016.
Printed in Singapore
by Tien Wah Press
First Edition
10 9 8 7 6 5 4 3 2 1

Library of Congress   96B2881
Cataloging-in-Publication Data

Reiser, Lynn.
Bedtime cat /
by Lynn Reiser.
p.   cm.
Summary: Child and cat
prepare for bedtime,
and suddenly the cat
disappears from sight.
ISBN 0-688-10025-2.
ISBN 0-688-10026-0 (lib. bdg.)
[1. Cats—Fiction.
2. Bedtime—Fiction.]
I. Title.
PZ7.R27745Be 1991
[E]—dc20
90-3883   CIP   AC

FOR

BISCUIT

AND

ALEXANDRA LYNN

THEIR STORY

When I come home,

my cat is waiting.

It's playtime   and reading time

and dinnertime for me and my cat.

It's
washing time

and

nightgown time

and

brushing time

and

bedtime

for me and my cat.

Where is my cat?

Having
a snack?

No.

Taking
a nap?

No.

Watching
the moon?

No.

Is my cat HIDING?

In the cupboard?

On the bookshelf?

Under the chair?

In the wastebasket?

No—
not in
the cupboard.

No—
not on
the bookshelf.

No—
not under
the chair.

No—
not in
the wastebasket.

WHERE

IS

MY

CAT?

Is my cat

outside —

IN THE DARK?

My cat is lost.

OH!

WHAT IS THAT?

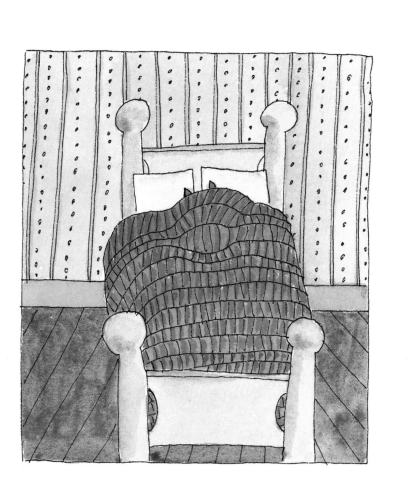

My cat is waiting.

It's bedtime for me and my cat.

Good night.